SPROUT S
NEIGHBORS

Five Stories

BOOK 1

24

WELCOME

ANNA ALTER

A YEARLING BOOK

For my sweet Tilly

All rights reserved. Published in the United States by Yearling, an imprint of Random House Children's Books, a division of Penguin Random House LLC, New York. Originally published in hardcover in the United States by Alfred A. Knopf, an imprint of Random House Children's Books, New York, in 2015.

Yearling and the jumping horse design are registered trademarks of Penguin Random House LLC.

Visit us on the Web! randomhousekids.com

Educators and librarians, for a variety of teaching tools, visit us at RHTeachersLibrarians.com

The Library of Congress has cataloged the hardcover edition of this work as follows:
Alter, Anna, author, illustrator.
Five stories / Anna Alter. — First edition.
p. cm. — (Sprout Street neighbors ; 1)
Summary: Relates the adventures of the animal residents of an apartment building on Sprout Street.
ISBN 978-0-385-75558-0 (trade) — ISBN 978-0-385-75559-7 (lib. bdg.) — ISBN 978-0-385-75561-0 (ebook)
[1. Neighbors—Fiction. 2. Apartment houses—Fiction. 3. Animals—Fiction.]
I. Title.
PZ7.A4635Fi 2015 [Fic]—dc23 2014000543

ISBN 978-0-385-75560-3 (pbk.)

Printed in the United States of America
10 9 8 7 6 5 4 3 2 1
First Yearling Edition 2016

CONTENTS

CHAPTER 1

The Acorn Problem

Henry lay in bed under his favorite quilt. It was the first day of fall and his room was chilly. He gazed out the window and watched his neighbors at 24 Sprout Street sweeping the walkway, raking the leaves, and doing their other weekend chores.

"What a waste of a Saturday morning," he thought. Stretching, he burrowed deeper into his quilt. He closed his eyes and began to drift asleep. Without warning, a loud *THUNK* shook him awake.

"What on earth could that be?" thought Henry. He pulled the covers over his nose. Then again, *THUNK*. "It's rather early to be so nois—" *THUNK*.

"Enough!" he grumbled, climbing out of bed and walking to the window. He saw nothing falling out of the sky that could make such a racket.

Henry put on his robe and stomped outside and into the yard. He looked around. His next-door neighbor, Wilbur, was raking red, orange, and yellow leaves. His third-floor neighbor, Violet, sat on the stoop knitting. Next to her was a basket full of colorful winter hats.

"Excuse me," he said. "Have either of you heard a loud thunking noise this morning?"

Wilbur stopped rak-
ing and looked up. "I
don't think so," he said.

"Me either," chirped
Violet.

Henry sighed. He turned around to go back
inside, but stopped in the doorway.

"Why have you knit so many hats?" he asked
Violet.

"They're all I know how to make," she said,
"and there is nothing more relaxing than knitting."

"Oh," said Henry, stepping inside.

Back in his apartment, it was nice and quiet
again. Henry yawned. He took off his robe and
climbed into bed. Outside his window, he could
see the wind gently lifting the leaves on the
trees. He thought about Violet and her rainbow
of hats. His eyes closed for a moment.

THUNK!

"Too much!" he cried as he leapt out of bed. He quickly got dressed and flew up the stairwell. Surely his second-floor neighbor Emma would know what was going on.

Henry stood in front of apartment 2A and raised his paw. But before he could knock on the door, the door knocked at him with a loud *THUNK-A-DUNK-DUNK.*

"Emma?" he called out.

"Come in!" Emma shouted from inside.

Henry pushed against the door. It opened halfway, then got stuck. He pulled the door closed again, then gave it a big push. *WHACK.*

Something was behind the door, and Henry had just hit it very hard. He squeezed through the doorway and his jaw dropped. Before him was the largest pile of acorns he had ever seen. And they were starting to move.

First, the acorns at the bottom of the pile began to shake. Next, the acorns in the middle started to jump. Then the acorns at the top started bouncing like popcorn. They bounced around so much that they all began rolling down, one after the other. Before he knew it, the entire pile landed on top of him. *THUNK THUNK THUNK THUNK THUNK . . .*

"Mystery solved," thought Henry from the bottom of the pile of acorns.

"Henry!" cried Emma, reaching through the nuts to help him up. "Are you all right?"

"Emma . . . ," he began. "Emma, I very much enjoy being your neighbor, but I must—"

"Oh, me too," she burst out. "You're simply

8

the best! I consider myself very lucky to be your neighbor. I really must have you over for lunch very soon."

"Yes," said Henry, standing up. He took a deep breath to tell her why he had come, but when he opened his mouth, nothing came out. He couldn't bring himself to tell her how much noise she was making.

Emma turned around and began stacking her acorns back into a pile. "I will invite you over just as soon as I finish moving things around," she went on. "Wilbur brought me all these acorns from the yard, and I simply don't have enough places to put them."

"Yes," said Henry again. "I can see that." Henry brushed off his pants and sighed. He wished her luck and returned downstairs.

Henry tried to forget about the noise. He

made some toast and opened a book of poetry. *THUNK!* His toast fell into his lap.

He put on some music and got out his playing cards. *THUNK!* His cards went flying.

He sat at his desk and tried to write a letter. *THUNK!* His pen scribbled straight off the page.

It wasn't working. Henry could not forget. So he put on his coat and went outside once more. Violet was still sitting on the stoop knitting. Her stack of hats was higher than it had been that morning.

"Hi, Violet," he said.

"Hi, Henry," Violet said. "Did you figure out what was making the thunking noise?"

"Oh, it was nothing," he said. "I'm going for a walk. See you later, Violet."

He left the porch and walked down Sprout Street. It was a clear day and the air smelled like cedar trees. Henry passed a garden full of yellow sunflowers and cheerful orange chrysanthemums. He gave a great yawn.

"Hello, Henry!" shouted a voice from across the street. He looked up to see Fernando, who lived across the hall from Violet. Fernando was heading home with two large bags in his paws.

"What are you up to?" called Henry.

"Just a little shopping," said Fernando. "I have a large loaf of bread and some good cheese in my bag. Care to join me for a bite to eat?"

12

"Yes, please," said Henry. With all the noise, he had forgotten to eat lunch.

He took a bag from his friend and they walked to 24 Sprout Street. Fernando told Henry about the cabbage soup and roasted potatoes he planned to make for dinner.

Henry suggested they sit under the oak tree in the yard. "It's freshly raked and there are no acorns at all," he pointed out.

After a few minutes, Violet came over to join them with her basket of hats. They sat under the tree together, eating the bread and cheese and chatting. Now and then, Violet picked up her knitting and added a hat to her stack.

Henry glanced up at Emma's window. He could see her stuffing acorns in cupboards and under chairs.  "I'm glad I'm not in my apartment," he thought. "There's got to be a lot of thunking going on." He yawned again.

"You seem tired," said Fernando, placing a large piece of cheese on a thick slice of bread.

"Yes," said Violet. "Did the thunking noise wake you up this morning?"

"To tell the truth, yes," Henry

sighed. "Emma has an apartment full of acorns and she's dropping them all over the place. I missed my morning nap completely."

"What a shame," said Violet.

They all sat quietly for a moment. Violet looked up at Emma, moving about in her apartment. Then she looked down at her hats—and got an idea. "Henry," she began, "do you think you might want to have some of my hats?"

"Thank you, Violet,"

said Henry, "but I'm not sure how that will help me get some sleep. Besides, my birthday isn't until October."

"Well, I have more than I can use," said Violet. "Perhaps you could give them to Emma."

After a bit of explaining and a lot of thanks, Henry returned to his apartment with a large stack of hats under his arm. He laid them on his bed and got out a box and some tissue paper.

 He put the hats in the box, wrapped them carefully, and tied a big bow around the outside. Then he went upstairs.

When Henry reached the top of the stairs, he heard a loud *CRACKITY THUNK-DUNK-DUNK*. A large acorn rolled straight out of Emma's front door and landed at his feet. He picked it up and went inside.

"Emma," Henry called out, "I have something for you!"

"Thank you," she said, "but I don't need any more acorns."

"Not this," he said, putting the acorn down and raising the box. "This!"

"Oh," Emma gasped, "but it's not my birthday until December!"

"I thought I would give you your present now," said Henry.

Emma dropped the three acorns she was carrying. *THUNK! THUNK! THUNK!* She picked up the box and tore open the package. "My," she said, "what lovely hats!"

"Violet made them," said Henry, "but they're not hats. They're acorn holders. Here, I'll show you."

Henry turned a hat upside down, picked up an acorn, and placed it inside. Then he tied the earflaps neatly to the back of a chair.

"Genius!" shouted Emma. "How clever! I am so lucky to have you as a friend."

"Not at all," said Henry, breathing a sigh of relief. "It is I who am lucky to have such wonderful friends."

Henry helped Emma put away her acorns, then went back downstairs and put on his pajamas. He had a long, peaceful afternoon nap and didn't get out of bed until it was time for supper.

CHAPTER 2

The Best Birthday

Emma could hardly sit still. She tapped her fingers on the kitchen table and swung her legs back and forth. Outside, snowflakes piled up on her windowsill. Soon it would be her birthday. The thought bounced happily in her head like a game of jacks.

She began pacing around the room, thinking of all the birthday parties she'd been to that year. At Fernando's party, there had been a clown to make jokes and hand out candy. At Henry's birthday, a magician did magic tricks and even pulled a rabbit out of a hat.

"I'll throw a party, too," thought Emma. "I'll invite everyone at 24 Sprout Street. It will be the best birthday ever!" She spun around and did a little *happy-birthday-to-me* dance.

Then Emma got very still. She needed to do something big to impress her friends. Something VERY big. She put on her coat, grabbed her thinking cap, and went downstairs to the front stoop, her favorite thinking spot.

Violet came through the door, carrying a shopping bag. "Good morning, Emma," she said. "What is that you're wearing on your head?"

"This is my thinking cap," said Emma.

"What are you thinking about?" asked Violet.

"Next week is my birthday and I want it to be the best birthday ever."

"Then I would have lots of balloons," suggested Violet.

"Yes!" cried Emma, jumping up and waving her thinking cap over her head. "The best birthday ever would surely have a lot of balloons! Thank you, Violet."

Emma shoved her thinking cap in her pocket and headed down Sprout Street toward Maple Street. She climbed the icy hill to Sergio's Market, where she bought a balloon

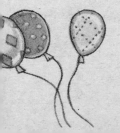

in every color. There was a bright red balloon the color of a summer tomato, an orange balloon as bright as a tangerine, and a magenta balloon the color of the bougainvillea in Wilbur's garden.

When she got home, Emma laid them all out on the table in her kitchen. They looked beautiful. She imagined them blown up, big and shiny, at her party.

But then she began to worry. Maybe her

friends wouldn't like the balloons. They weren't as special as a clown or a magician. She would have to think a lot harder if she wanted this to be the best birthday ever.

So Emma put on her thinking cap again. This time, she sat in her sunroom, tapping her toes on the tile and watching the snow fall. *"Think,"* she said to herself.

Rrrrr-ing! rang the phone.

"Oh, hello, Wilbur. Yes, it is really coming down outside. Wilbur, can I ask you something?"

"Of course," said Wilbur on the other end.

"What would you do to make a birthday the best birthday ever?"

"Well..." He paused for a

27

moment. "At my birthday party last year, we had a piñata. That was my best birthday ever."

Emma smiled from ear to ear, remembering Wilbur's glittering, watermelon-shaped piñata swinging from the ceiling. She jumped out of her chair and threw her thinking cap into the air.

"A piñata, of course! Thank you, Wilbur!"

She hung up the phone and went back to Sergio's. There were so many piñatas hanging from the ceiling, it was hard to decide which was the best. Then she spotted a tall giraffe with blue spots and a tail

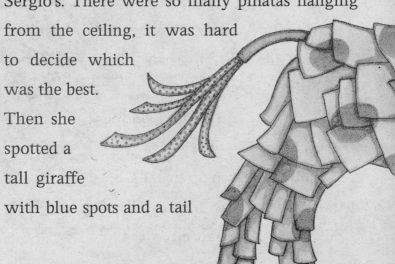

made out of sparkling streamers. "Perfect!" thought Emma.

On the way home, the snow stopped and the sky began to clear. Emma went inside and put the piñata on the table, next to the balloons. The streamers sparkled in the sunlight. Surely the best birthday ever would have a piñata like this one. She leaned back to admire it.

But then she started to worry again. "What if my friends don't like the piñata?" she thought. "What if they're tired of piñatas after Wilbur's party?" Emma sighed. She would have to go back to square one.

This time, she decided to go for a walk. She thought very hard. When she arrived at the bottom of the hill, she found herself in front of Sweetcakes, her favorite bakery.

The window was covered in frost. Emma wiped away a small circle and looked through the glass. The bakers were lifting cakes out of their pans, filling them with vanilla custard, covering them with velvety-smooth icing. Her mouth watered. Then her eyes wandered to the end of the counter, where a baker was hard at work piping small, beautiful pink roses.

Suddenly Emma got an idea. The biggest idea yet. "I know what will make my birthday the best ever," she couldn't help saying out loud.

"I will make a glorious birthday cake! It will be the biggest, most beautiful birthday cake anyone has ever seen. There will be fifteen layers and icing in every color of the rainbow. And at the top, a shiny, perfect acorn made out of marzipan!"

Emma ran back to Sprout Street and made invitations for all of her neighbors. When they were finished, she carried them to the corner outside and put them in the mailbox.

She skipped back to her apartment and got to work in the kitchen. She mixed, she poured, she whipped, and she frosted. Each morning, she put on her apron and added something new. Her cake climbed taller and taller, and grew more stunning by the day. She filled it with peaches, blueberries, and chestnut cream. Sprinkles covered the cake like dew and glimmered in the sunlight. Chocolate truffles lined the tiers. And on the top, the single perfect marzipan acorn sat like a queen on her throne.

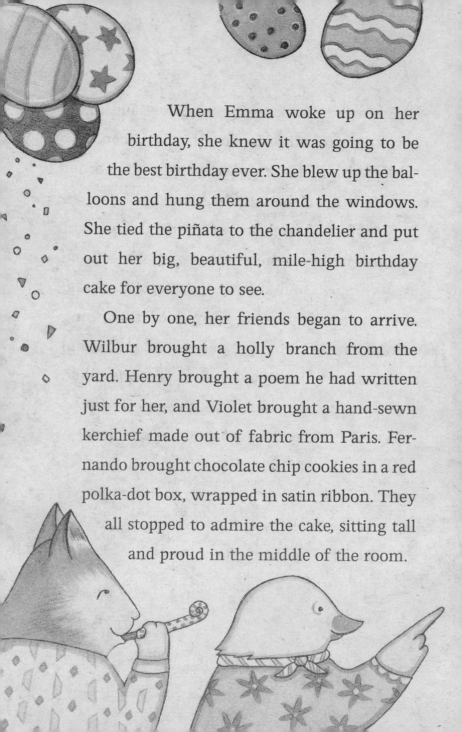

When Emma woke up on her birthday, she knew it was going to be the best birthday ever. She blew up the balloons and hung them around the windows. She tied the piñata to the chandelier and put out her big, beautiful, mile-high birthday cake for everyone to see.

One by one, her friends began to arrive. Wilbur brought a holly branch from the yard. Henry brought a poem he had written just for her, and Violet brought a hand-sewn kerchief made out of fabric from Paris. Fernando brought chocolate chip cookies in a red polka-dot box, wrapped in satin ribbon. They all stopped to admire the cake, sitting tall and proud in the middle of the room.

"Beautiful!" said Wilbur.

"Incredible!" said Henry.

"Absolutely perfect!" said Violet.

Fernando, awestruck, couldn't help reaching out for a little taste. Violet swooped in before he could get close enough and walked him to the punch bowl.

Everyone gathered around the piñata. Violet picked up the wooden paddle. Emma tied a blindfold over her eyes and turned her in a circle. Violet stretched the paddle behind her, then swung

it forward with all her might.
There was a *THUD* and then
a *THUMP* as the piñata hit
the wall without breaking.

Next, it was Henry's turn. He swung the
paddle, *swoosh*, through the air. He swung it so
hard that he lost his balance and slid across the
floor into a pile of balloons, *POP POP POP*.
Wilbur chuckled and helped Henry up.

Each neighbor at 24 Sprout Street had a try,

until at last it was Emma's turn. Fernando tied her blindfold and spun her round and round. Emma imagined all the candy that would rain down from the piñata—the perfect appetizer for her beautiful, incredible, absolutely perfect cake. She took a big, strong swing. *THWACK.*

It was a strange noise for a piñata to make. When she tried to move her paddle, it appeared to be stuck. She took the blindfold off her eyes.

Emma gasped. Her paddle was wedged deep inside the cake, which was now leaning toward the front door. *Creeeeeeeeeak* went the table as the cake began to sway. It leaned left, it leaned right, and then it toppled, layer by layer, into a heap on the floor.

Emma's heart sank first into her stomach, then into her shoes, then right down onto the floor and into a heap with the remains of her cake.

Wilbur looked at Emma. He scooped up a handful of icing and tasted it. "This is delicious," he said.

Violet grabbed a handful of cake and took a bite, too. "Best birthday cake I've ever had!" she declared.

Henry reached into the pile and picked up the shiny, perfect acorn. He pressed a candle into the

top and lit it. "Make a wish," he told
Emma, holding it in front of her.

Emma smiled. She made a wish
and blew out the candle.

Before long, everyone was sitting on
the floor, laughing and eating squashed
birthday cake. Wilbur put some icing on his
chin in the shape of a beard and shouted, "Ho,
ho, ho!" Fernando made a snowball out of

whipped cream and threw it at Henry's mouth. He missed and hit Violet on the wing.

"Now that's what I call a confection collision!" giggled Violet.

"A real frosting fiasco!" Fernando chimed in, laughing so hard, tears rolled down his cheeks.

Emma picked up a handful of chestnut cream and put it in her mouth. It tasted nutty and sweet. This wasn't exactly how she had imagined her best birthday ever, but it most certainly was.

"Emma's Poem"

by Henry

On my upstairs neighbor I've come to depend.

When I need some sugar, she's happy to lend.

When she throws a party, I want to attend.

This downstairs neighbor just loves to ascend.

I'm ever so glad for my upstairs friend!

CHAPTER 3

Fernando's Wish

One spring afternoon, Fernando sat in his living room, eating cherry pie and thinking about his secret wish. He could spend hours letting his wish swirl around inside him, like a moth looking for light. It thrilled him from head to toe. He crossed his legs at the knee and bounced his top foot.

Before long, a strange noise drifted in from across the hall and broke the silence.

Floo flooooo, sweeeeeeee!

Fernando knew exactly what that sound was.

Someone was practicing the flute for the Sprout Street Daffodil Parade, only a week away. And that someone was Violet.

She had convinced everyone in the building to play a part in the parade. Wilbur would make a float filled with flowers. Emma would do cartwheels with the marching band, and Henry had been writing a poem about springtime to read at the head of the parade.

Fernando hadn't decided what he would do. To be honest, the idea of marching in the parade made him nervous. What if he made a fool of himself? What if he tripped and his shoe went flying into the air? What if everyone then called him Mr. One-Shoe? The idea made him want to climb into bed and think about his wish all day.

Instead, Fernando walked out to the backyard, where Wilbur was working on his float. Little tufts of bright green grass had begun to poke out of the ground around him.

"I just don't know if I'm parade material," Fernando said, pacing back and forth.

"Of course you are," said Wilbur. He stood up to press a yellow-and-orange daffodil into a large chicken-wire frame. "Besides, you have to come. Everyone on Sprout Street is marching in the parade together."

"That's what I was afraid you'd say," sighed Fernando.

"Isn't there anything you want to do?" asked Wilbur.

Fernando blushed and thought briefly of his wish, but decided to leave it inside, where it was.

Wilbur looked at his float. Then he looked at Fernando. "Why don't you march as a daffodil?" he suggested. "It is, after all, the Daffodil Parade. You would be a great daffodil."

"I suppose I could do that," said Fernando.

Wilbur walked over to a basket and pulled out some extra chicken wire. He held it up to Fernando. The wire reached from his chin to his waist.

"Perfect!" he said. "Now all we need is some paper on the outside to turn it into a daffodil. Maybe Violet will help you?"

Feeee fee hoooooonk!

Fernando went to Violet's apartment and knocked on the door. He heard a *swaa sweeee* and then some shuffling.

Violet opened the door wide and smiled. "Hi, Fernando!"

"Hi," he said, shifting from one foot to the other, then back again. He held the chicken wire behind him.

"You really are getting better at the flute," he offered. Violet beamed, and some of the feathers on top of her head seemed to puff up slightly.

"I have a favor to ask. Do you have some paper I could use to cover this wire? Wilbur

49

thought I should be a daffodil in the parade, and I need a costume."

"What a clever idea," she said, waving him inside. She walked over to her craft corner and held up her wing. "Use whatever you like!" she chirped. "I'm happy to help."

Fernando marveled at her collection of art supplies. There was a carton full of glitter pens, an old pickle jar filled with crayon bits, and a cereal box with dozens of different kinds of ribbon curled inside.

Fernando stepped forward and pulled open a drawer. Inside was a stack of tissue paper in

every color he could imagine. It was so thin and soft. He picked up a sheet of lemon yellow and let it float in the air for a moment, like a ballerina sailing across the stage.

Violet took some newspaper and put it on the floor. From the kitchen, she brought out a bowl filled with flour and a pitcher of water.

"Are we baking a cake first?" asked Fernando hopefully.

"This is for the papier-mâché," said Violet. She poured the water into the flour and mixed it until it looked like pancake batter. "We'll dip the newspaper in here and then use it to cover the

chicken wire. When it hardens, we can decorate your costume so that it looks like a daffodil."

She picked up the chicken wire and tied it into a tube with some string. Then she tore up strips of newspaper, dipped them into the bowl, and smoothed them over the chicken wire.

"Give it a try," she said.

Fernando bent over the bowl and dipped in a piece of newspaper. He smoothed it onto the chicken wire, next to Violet's piece.

They worked and worked. Finally, the wire tube was covered in papier-mâché.

"We have to let this dry before we can put on the tissue paper," said Violet. "Let's go for a walk and we can do it when we get back."

By now, Fernando was feeling more relaxed. Maybe the parade wouldn't be so bad after all. He was also hungry, so he suggested they go to Sweet-cakes for a snack. They washed up and headed outside. He skipped a little as they got closer.

They sat in the front of the bakery, on either side of a large plate of chocolate chip cookies. Violet talked about how much she loved to play the flute. "I have wanted to play as long as I can remember," she said. "When I pick up my flute, it's like climbing into a hot-air balloon and sailing into the sky!"

Fernando thought about what that would feel like. Then, all at once, it felt as though the ground was shifting beneath him. He reached for his glass of milk and froze. The desire to let out his secret wish took hold. He didn't know how or why, but suddenly he had to say it, right this minute. He looked at Violet, who looked back at him.

"You seem a little pale," she noticed.

"Violet," he began, "there is something I have never told anyone, and I think I would like to tell you."

Violet took a bite of her cookie and gave a nod. Fernando took a breath.

"I WANT TO DANCE!" he cried. It bubbled out so quickly and from so deep down inside that he almost wasn't sure he'd said it at all.

Violet perked up and put her cookie down.

Fernando tried to get ahold of himself. "I mean . . . I really think I could dance, if I tried."

He began to wonder if he had made a mistake. Violet was going to think he was ridiculous. She would probably tell everyone that he was crazy and to stop being friends with him. He looked down at his feet.

Violet's eyes got wide. "Fantastic! Stupendous! You should dance, Fernando!"

Fernando lifted his head. He felt as big as a mountain and as light as a feather.

"Why don't you dance in the PARADE?" Violet went on, slapping her wings on her lap.

Fernando felt a little smaller. "Thank you, Violet, but I can't dance in the parade. I've never done anything like it before. Everyone will be watching."

"I don't know if you realize this," Violet said, "but I had never played the flute before last

week. I don't really know how. I'm just making it up as I go along."

Fernando and everyone at 24 Sprout Street knew that Violet did not know how to play the flute. But they would never tell her that.

"Aren't you afraid of playing in front of everyone?" he asked.

Violet shrugged. "Not anymore. I just think about how much I love to play, and then I don't care who's watching."

It was getting late in the afternoon, so they headed back home to finish the daffodil costume. Fernando was quiet as they added layers of green and yellow tissue paper, then sculpted a hat that looked like petals. At last, it was complete.

He carried his giant daffodil across the hall to his apartment. He placed it on the floor, giving it a hard look.

Violet began practicing her flute in her apartment again.

Feeee fee swooo!

Fernando stood up and closed his eyes. He could feel the music inside him, floating around like his wish. Before he could give it a second thought, his foot started tapping beneath him. He looked down. Slowly, his knees began to bend.

Swa swa fleeeee, the flute went on.

The rhythm took over his hips, then moved into his arms. They reached down to the ground, then high up into the air, shifting back and forth gracefully like a tree branch in the wind.

"I am dancing," he said out loud. "I am really dancing!"

Fernando danced and danced. He did pliés

and high kicks and lightning-fast spins. His paws fluttered through the air like butterflies. His feet moved so fast, they were a blur beneath him.

Violet stopped playing her flute, but he kept right on dancing, faster and faster. He felt like a sea of daffodils, bobbing and swaying in the wind.

One morning the following week, before the sun came in through anyone's window, Fernando, Wilbur, Emma, and Henry were woken up by a loud *fwee fwee squeeee* coming from the hallway. Violet was running up and down the stairs of the building, giving everyone a preview of her Daffodil Parade performance.

Wilbur rolled out of bed and made a cup of orange blossom tea.

Emma cartwheeled out of bed and into her Daffodil Parade dress. Henry cleared his throat and began to practice his poem. And Fernando slid into his slippers with a double pirouette, pretending he was a brand-new daffodil, waiting to greet the sun.

As the rest of the neighborhood began to gather on the lawn, the parade got ready behind the azalea bushes. Henry stood proudly at the front, holding his poem like a flag for all to see.

Emma was getting in a few last practice cart-wheels while the tuba player rehearsed. Violet was squealing away on the flute, and Wilbur stood at the helm of his float: a fire-breathing dragon built completely out of flowers.

Fernando climbed into his daffodil costume and looked around. He watched everyone in the parade ahead of him getting ready to march. In the distance, he could see the waiting crowd. Just then, his knees felt weak.

Fwee feeeeee whooooo!

The sound of Violet's flute brought him back.

He closed his eyes and imagined what a daffodil might feel
on a day like today. A daffodil
would be proud and happy to feel
the sun on its face. Fernando
stood up a little taller.

The band got into formation and
began to play. Before he knew it,
Fernando's feet were marching in time,
and he was dancing down Sprout
Street, stepping and swaying like a daffodil welcoming the spring.

The crowd cheered and shouted.

But all Fernando could hear
was the slow, steady beat of a
most beautiful melody un-
folding deep within him.

CHAPTER 4

The Surprise

Violet walked into her bathroom and opened the window next to the sink. A warm early-summer breeze drifted in, carrying the sound of a family of sparrows singing outside. She loved living on the top floor of 24 Sprout Street, close to her feathered cousins.

Violet looked in her bathroom mirror and grinned. She picked up her toothbrush, covered it in toothpaste, and lifted it to her mouth.

Plink!

She froze. "Sparrows do not say *plink!*" she thought. Just then, a single drop of water rolled down her forehead and onto her beak. She squinted at the ceiling. Above her head, there was a small yellow circle, the size of a lemon.

Plink!

Another drop rained down, this time hitting her right between the eyes. Violet blinked. She walked into the kitchen, took out a teacup, and placed it beneath the leak.

Violet finished brushing her teeth, left the bathroom, and settled into her reading chair. She picked up her copy of *A Guide to Backyard Birds* and opened to chapter three, "The Way of the Woodpecker."

Plunk!

This time, a drop of water landed on page twenty-six, then slid down onto her lap. She looked up. Above her was another yellow stain, this one the size of a grapefruit.

Violet got up, pushed her chair forward a few feet, and placed a salad bowl under the leak. "That should do it," she said to herself.

She picked up her book again and the room fell away. All around her were a flock of woodpeckers, fluttering here and there, looking for a place to nest. Just then, she heard a knock, like a woodpecker tapping on a tree. Violet went to her front door and opened it.

"Hello, Henry," she said.

"Hi, Violet," said Henry. "May I come in?"

She stepped back and opened the door wider. Henry came in and looked around. His eyes lingered at the kitchen door.

"I'm just out of jam," he began. "I wonder if I might borrow—"

Plink!

Something smacked him on the shoulder. He looked at the soggy spot on his sweater, then up at the ceiling.

"You have a leak!" he said, stepping aside.

"Yes, sorry, just a moment," said Violet.

She went into the kitchen, picked up a saucer, and brought it back to the living room. She placed it where Henry had been standing, and the water fell, *plink! plink! plunk!*, into the dish.

"Perhaps you should call for some help?" suggested Henry, sitting down on the sofa.

"Thanks," said Violet, "but I can take care of this by myself." Taking care of things was something Violet was very good at.

Water dripped from the ceiling and fell, *plink! plunk!*, into the dishes spread around the apartment, like a summer rainstorm.

"I see," he said.

"Make yourself comfortable," said Violet. "I'll fix us some jam and toast."

She went into the kitchen and took out the strawberry jam. As she reached for a loaf of bread from the cupboard, something went *plink!* behind her. She spun around to see water dripping into the flour bin.

"Oh no!" she cried, racing to move it out of the way. Now the drops were falling on the counter. She moved an empty sugar bowl to catch them.

"Is everything okay in there?" called Henry from the living room.

"Oh yes, fine!" shouted Violet. "I'll just be a minute!"

Violet stepped away from the counter and felt something wet on her foot. She looked

up and spied another grapefruit on the ceiling.
This time, she put a soup bowl on the floor.

"Let me help you!" said Henry in the other room, getting up.

Violet could hear him walking toward the kitchen. She took a step to reach for the jam, but the floor began to move beneath her. The soup bowl spun out from under her foot, and Violet fell, *WHUMP*, flat on her back.

Tiny drops of water were now falling onto her chin. She closed her eyes. "Maybe if I keep them shut long enough, everything will go back to normal," she thought.

A few moments later, she opened one eye to see if it was working. There was Henry, leaning over her with a frown.

"Are you all right?" he asked.

"Of course!" she said a little too loudly. "Why do you ask?" Violet stood up and limped into a kitchen chair.

Henry looked around. "There's water leaking everywhere," he said. "You should call Ms. Thornbush. Her fix-it shop is just down the street."

"It's okay," said Violet, clearing her throat. "I can manage." She reached for a dish towel and dried her face.

"Let's eat outside," Henry sighed. "The weather might be a bit better than it is in here."

"All right," agreed Violet.

She put the jam and bread in a bag. They

walked downstairs to the front
porch of 24 Sprout Street and sat
on the swing.

Just then, Wilbur climbed
the front steps. He was carrying a basket full of blueberries from the bushes
in the yard. He nodded
to his neighbors and
held out the basket.

"What brings you
two down here this morning?" he asked.

"My apartment is a little
wet," Violet said, reaching for
a berry.

"*A little?*" scoffed Henry. "The
roof is leaking like a faucet!"

"It's not so bad," said Violet, popping the berry into her mouth. "I have it all under control."

Wilbur looked at Henry, then back at Violet. "Well, stop by anytime you need to dry off," he said, heading inside.

After breakfast, Violet went back upstairs and lay down on the couch. Her eyes felt heavy. The drops of water plinking and plunking around her sounded like a lullaby. Soon she was asleep.

When she opened her eyes again, it was late afternoon. Violet wasn't quite sure where she was. She was lying on what looked like her couch, but it was bobbing up and down, like a log on a river.

She peered over the edge. There was water as far as she could see. Shoes floated by like little boats. "Oh dear!" she cried.

A broom floated near the end of the couch. Violet sprang to her knees and pulled it onto the cushions. Holding it like a paddle, she rowed the couch to the front door and turned the handle.

WHOOSH!

Water lifted the sofa into the hallway, then escaped down the stairs. Violet hopped off the sofa, ran back to the door, and closed it quickly.

She stood for a moment and tried to collect herself. "Maybe I *will* pay Wilbur a visit after all," she decided.

She went downstairs and knocked on Wilbur's door. Taking a breath, she tried to think of what to say. Water dripped from her pants down onto the doormat.

Wilbur opened the door and looked her up and down. "Violet! Just who I was hoping to see. I could use your help."

Violet put her wings in her soaked pockets. "You could?" she asked.

"I need to water the blueberry bushes in the

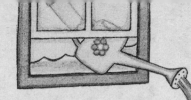

yard, and the hose won't reach. Might I borrow some of the water in your apartment?"

"Of course!" said Violet, beaming.

They went upstairs together, carrying two large watering cans. Wilbur sloshed through the living room and opened a window. He leaned out and looked down. "Perfect!" he said, dipping his watering can into the pool around him and filling it up. He held it out the window, and the water rained down on the bushes below. Violet smiled and splish-splashed over to help.

Within the hour, Violet's shoes were no longer floating around the room, and they could see the floor again. But drops of water still plink-plunked from above.

"You have been such an enormous help," Wilbur declared, "you must let me find a way to thank you."

Violet blushed. "You don't have to."

"Please," he said, "let me do something for you. A surprise."

"All right," said Violet.

Wilbur went downstairs and Violet walked around the room, placing her dishes back beneath the drips. Before long, there was a knock at the door.

"Have a seat and close your eyes!" shouted Wilbur from the hallway.

Violet sat down on her reading chair. *Squish.* Water oozed out of the cushions and dripped onto her toes. She closed her eyes.

The door opened and she heard footsteps moving around the room. There was a *clank clank clank* that sounded like someone climbing a ladder. There was the

THUD of a hammer hitting wood, and once in a while a loud *ca-LUNK*. Violet sat patiently and waited.

Suddenly it was quiet. Not even a *plink! plink!* broke the silence. She could take it no longer and opened her eyes.

There was not a drop of water in sight. Wilbur and Henry were putting the couch back in place. Ms. Thornbush was picking up her toolbox. Violet was too stunned to speak. Henry gave her a wink as he folded up the ladder.

"Surprise!" Wilbur said. "The leak in your ceiling is fixed! Shall we go down to my place to celebrate? I have a blueberry pie just out of the oven. I can't eat the whole thing by myself."

Henry perked up at the mention of pie. "Sounds good to me!" he chimed in.

Violet looked at Wilbur and smiled. "I just need a moment to dry off," she said shyly.

Wilbur and Henry went downstairs and Violet sat glued to her chair. She closed her eyes again. This time, she was not wishing away the leaky ceiling or waiting for a surprise. She was just enjoying the quiet. "I might not know how to fix a leak," she thought, "but I know how to choose a good friend."

CHAPTER 5

The Secret Garden

Wilbur put on a wide-brimmed hat to shade his face from the late-summer sun. He placed his hand shovel in his back pocket and began to walk across the yard of 24 Sprout Street. It was early. The birds had just begun to chatter in the treetops, and there was a chill in the air. It smelled like fresh-cut grass.

When he was half a block past Sergio's Market, he turned, passing through an old, crooked gate. He lifted his head and took a deep breath.

The smell of his garden in full bloom filled his chest and lifted him up. He couldn't wait to feel the damp soil on his paws and the sun on the fur at the back of his neck.

He watered the hydrangeas, picked the basil, and gathered some tiger lilies. As he worked throughout the day, the sweet smell on his finger-tips made his heart flutter.

Emma often strolled down Maple Street after stopping at the market. Today, she stopped in front of Wilbur's garden and peered over the fence.

"Hi there, Wilbur!" she called out.

Wilbur looked up. Was there a bird chirping

in the sky above him? Not seeing any, he got back to work.

"HI THERE, WILBUR!" Emma repeated at the top of her lungs.

Suddenly he had the feeling that he wasn't alone. He searched the edge of his plot, where he found Emma's face beaming at him.

"Oh, good morning, Emma! I didn't see you there."

"It's four o'clock, neighbor, not morning at all. You should take a break once in a while!" Emma's eyes twinkled as she turned to go.

Wilbur smiled. How could the day have gone by so quickly? His shadow stretched long over the

rosebushes. Time to head home
and start supper. He picked up his
shovel, put the lilies and basil in a
basket, then walked over to the gate.

When he reached Sergio's, he stopped to peer
through the window. Inside, Sergio was selling
Henry some barley seeds. Behind Henry was a
long line of people wedged in a crowded aisle,
waiting to buy their groceries.

"Bit of a tight squeeze," he thought.

As he turned to go, a sign on the front door
caught his eye:

"Well, it's about time," Wilbur thought, heading home.

Suddenly he stopped in his tracks. That address sounded familiar. He turned around, dropping the basket, and ran to his garden as quickly as his legs would take him. When he got there, his heart sank. The numbers 5, 3, and 6 hung loosely on the gate under a post, in rusted iron.

How could Sergio move into his garden? Someone in his family had been gardening in that spot as long as he could remember. First was Grandma Gertrude, who had passed by the empty lot one day and noticed the black soil, perfect for planting. She had worked the garden there for many years, then passed it on to his cousin Charlie. Charlie had given it to crazy Aunt Petunia, who had tried to plant chocolate chips and grow a cookie tree. Crazy Aunt Petunia had given it to him.

Wilbur hurried home, sprinting past Violet and Fernando, who were chatting on the front stoop. He heard "more space for sunflower seeds" and "new grapefruit display" float through the air as he rushed past.

Back in the comfort of his apartment, he walked over to his pantry. He opened the doors and looked inside. The shelves were lined with food from his garden: dried herbs, jars of tomatoes and pepper jelly, strawberry jam, and chamomile blossoms. His pantry looked like an aisle in a grocery store. Sergio's grocery store. Wilbur sighed.

There was a knock at the door. He opened it a crack and peered through. Fernando stood on the other side. His arms were crossed.

"Wilbur," he began, "what's wrong? You went by in such a rush."

Wilbur took a breath, but he couldn't think straight. His heart was in his throat.

"Sergio . . . my hydrangeas . . . chocolate chips!" he choked out.

93

Fernando looked confused. "I'm sorry, Wilbur, but I don't understand." He had never seen Wilbur so upset about anything.

"Grandma Gertrude, rosebushes, new location in September!" he continued.

Fernando was even more confused.

"I'm sorry," Wilbur said. "I need to be alone." He sighed again and shut the door.

Wilbur sat in his grandma's rocker and looked out the window. The more he thought of the zinnias that would never flower and the roses that would wither, the worse he felt. His eyes started to grow heavy, so he rested his head on the side of the chair.

Something tugged at his foot. He looked down and saw a green vine curling out of the floorboards and wrapping around his ankles. It twisted and curled, slowly but tightly, tying him to his chair.

Wilbur began to lift his paws to free his legs, but they wouldn't budge. They, too, were tied to the chair by the creeping vine, moving more swiftly as the minutes passed.

A knock at the door woke him and he jumped to his feet. When he looked down, there was no vine in sight. "It must have been a dream," he thought. "Perhaps it all was. Perhaps Sergio's was never going to move in the first place."

He shook himself the rest of the way awake and walked to the front door. When he opened it, Fernando was there again, this time with something in his hands.

"For you," he said, handing him a plate of peanut butter cookies. "A sweet end to a sour day."

Wilbur smiled. "Thank you, Fernando. Would you like to come in?"

"Yes, thank you," he said.

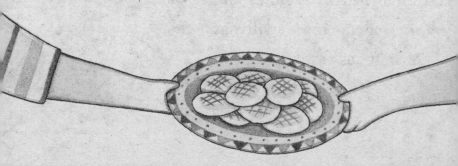

They sat together by the window and drank warm milk with their cookies. Wilbur explained what he'd been through that day and why he had been so upset earlier. As he spoke, Fernando said things like "You don't say!" and "Dreadful!" and "I don't believe it!" Wilbur was very relieved to have his thoughts off his chest.

The next day before the sun rose, he woke up to a strange birdcall. *Eeeeeep eeeeeep* sounded over and over from the window. When he sat up and peered outside, his face fell. It was no bird making that noise, but a tractor heading in the direction of his garden.

He threw on his clothes, grabbed his jacket,

and ran for the door. As he raced down the hall, he nearly toppled over an empty plastic bucket. "Not the best place for that," he thought.

He continued through the foyer and reached for the front door. Looking down, he noticed a large pile of dirt by the doormat. "Strange," he thought. "I wonder who left such a mess."

Eeeeeep eeeeeep sounded again from the street. Shutting the door behind him, he ran quickly toward Maple Street.

Today was quieter than usual. The sky was dark and the birds still slept in their nests. But when Wilbur arrived at the next block, the quiet came to an end.

There were people moving back and forth in front of 536 Maple Street—hanging signs, unloading shovels, and calling out to one another. A large yellow digger was parked beside the gate.

"It wasn't a dream," said Wilbur to no one in particular. He couldn't bear to look over the fence and see what was on the other side. He simply turned around and headed home.

When he arrived at 24 Sprout Street, the sun had begun to peek out from behind the building. He could see Fernando and Henry on the porch swing. "Good morning, Wilbur!" they shouted as he crossed the yard. Wilbur couldn't bring himself to reply.

"Wilbur," said Fernando, "we've been

looking for you everywhere. We have something to show you."

"I'm not in the mood," he said.

"Just follow me," said Fernando, hopping to his feet.

Henry yawned and Wilbur noticed something strange. Henry's shoes, usually so clean and tidy, were covered in dirt.

"Okay," he said.

He followed Fernando and Henry up the stairs. They passed Henry's door on the first floor and Emma's on the second. When they got to Fernando's door on the third floor, Wilbur stopped, expecting him to open it.

"We're not going in there," Fernando said. "Come this way."

They climbed one more flight of stairs, and Henry opened the door to the roof. Wilbur followed Fernando through the door, looking down at his feet.

Out of the corner of his eye, he thought he caught a glimpse of something purple. He could have sworn he saw Grandma Gertrude's butterfly bushes. Wilbur lifted his head and gasped. "My garden!"

All around him were his oregano plants, cherry tomatoes, and geraniums, carefully planted in white buckets. Bees buzzed around their blossoms as they swayed in the breeze. He couldn't believe his eyes.

Henry and Fernando joined Violet and Emma, who were standing in a corner,

drinking iced tea. Henry yawned again and Emma rubbed her eyes. They all looked very, very tired.

"Thank you," said Wilbur softly. "You must have been up all night. This is the nicest thing anyone has ever done for me."

Violet smiled, took his arm, and brought him over to a hammock underneath a lilac tree. Everyone settled in and recalled for Wilbur, in

great detail, the long night of digging and planting. He asked again and again how they had carefully lifted each plant out of the ground.

"Sergio gave us the buckets," said Fernando.

"We passed them to each other up all three
flights of stairs at 24 Sprout Street," said Emma.

"We had to work through the night," Henry
added.

"And without a sound," said Violet, "so as not
to spoil the surprise."

Then, one by one, the neighbors closed their
eyes for a long morning nap. All except for Wilbur, who was too excited to sleep. He gazed
gratefully at his friends, and then rested his eyes
on his hydrangea bushes until the sun climbed
high into the sky.

**Meet the newest Sprout Street neighbor
in this special sneak peek!**

CHAPTER 1

Apartment 2B

The sky poured rain onto 24 Sprout Street. Violet sat on the porch swing and reached into her basket. "This will do nicely," she said, picking up a ball of yellow wool. The swing rocked back and forth. She listened to the rain pitter patter on the roof, then splash down onto the azalea bushes.

Screeeeeech! Violet jumped, falling out of her seat. She walked to the stoop to see what was making such a terrible noise. A truck pulled close to the sidewalk, then stopped in front of the building.

Just then, the wind picked up and sprayed water on Violet's feet. A chill climbed up her back and made her feathers stand on end. *"Ah-CHOO!"* Violet sneezed.

A small figure got out of the truck and opened a large umbrella. Violet squinted her eyes. All she could see of the stranger was a yellow raincoat and a pair of green galoshes.

"Ah-CHOO!" Violet sneezed again.

She was getting drenched, so she picked up her knitting and went inside. On the landing she found Henry, sitting on a step and muttering to himself.

"Hi, Hen— *Ah-CHOO!*"
sneezed Violet.

"There you are!" said
Henry. "I was just coming
to see you. I need your help.
My trench coat has a tear
and needs mending."

Everyone at 24 Sprout Street
depended on Violet to mend their clothes. It
seemed there was nothing she couldn't fix.

"Of course," she said, stepping toward him,
ker-splish ker-splosh. She looked down. "Perhaps
I better just change my clothes first."

Once inside her apartment, Violet put on a
dry sweater, a skirt, and some wool socks.

"*Ah-CHOO!*" she sneezed.

When she took out her hankie to blow her
nose, it felt as if her head was spinning. She

grabbed on to a kitchen chair to get her balance, then wobbled into the hallway to look for Henry.

Leaning over the railing, she peered down the steps. In front of apartment 2B, directly across from Emma's, was a pair of green galoshes, shiny with raindrops. No one had lived in that apartment for so long, Violet had almost forgotten it was there.

If she was going to have a new neighbor, a warm welcome was in order. Violet went back inside her apartment and pulled out a piece of paper. She picked up a marker and wrote *WELCOME* in big red letters across the top. Underneath it, she drew a picture of the oak tree in the yard, filled with leaves and acorns. At the bottom, she signed her name.

Violet gazed at her work of art and began to imagine what the new neighbor would be like. Maybe she would like to write poetry, like Henry, or plant rosebushes, like Wilbur?

There was a knock at the door. Before she could answer, Emma burst through with her paws in the air.

"Violet! Did you HEAR? I have a new neighbor. WE  have a new neighbor. She is moving in downstairs as we speak!"

"Yes," said Violet. "I saw her galoshes."

"We should go welcome her, don't you think? Yes, yes, we should. Let's go now!"

"*Ah-CHOO!*" said Violet. "Yes, let's." She

put her drawing in her pocket and walked downstairs with Emma, who knocked at apartment 2B.

At first, there was no answer. But then they heard the *slush-slush-slide* of boxes being pushed along the floor. Slowly, the doorknob turned. The door opened just enough for a pointy nose to peek through and give a sniff.

"Hello!" said Emma. "We are your new neighbors, Emma and Violet. We've come to welcome you to the building!"

The nose went back inside. Then the door opened wide and a face appeared around it. Two round eyes blinked from beneath a fancy blue beret. The new neighbor reached up to slide the hat off her head, and her mouth curled into a smile.

"Thank you," she giggled. "My name is Mililani, but you can call me Mili. Please come in!"

Emma and Violet followed Mili into her living room, filled with boxes piled to the ceiling. They looked like cardboard skyscrapers. In the middle of the room was a metal bin holding a stack of framed pictures.

"What's in here?" Violet asked.

"Those are my paintings," said Mili.

"I am something of an artist myself," said Violet, perking up. "May I see?"

"Sure," said Mili, walking to the bin and pulling a painting out from the middle of the stack. It was a picture of a rocky beach surrounded by palm trees. The sky above was a brilliant blue. In the distance, a volcano sent smoke winding up into the soft, feathery clouds. It looked so real, you could almost reach out and touch it.

Emma's jaw dropped. "You are so talented! Isn't she talented, Violet?"

Violet's eyes got wide and her cheeks turned pink. She felt a tiny pinch in her stomach. "It's very nice," she peeped.

"Thanks," said Mili. "It's a picture of the view from my old apartment in Hawaii."

Violet reached into her pocket and wrapped

her wing around her drawing, squeezing it into a little crumpled ball. She cleared her throat.

"I'm afraid I'm a little under the weather today. I'll have to join you another time. Welcome to the building, Mili." She rushed out the door.

Hurrying through the hallway, Violet couldn't bring herself to look up from her feet, until—*THUD*—she crashed into something and lifted her eyes.

"Oh! I'm sorry, Henry! I didn't see you there!" she cried.

"That's all right, I suppose." Henry made a big show of pulling himself up off the floor.

"I'm glad we ran into each other." She smiled. "You can give me your trench coat to mend."

"Never mind about that," said Henry. "I met our new neighbor and she offered to do it."

Violet's stomach pinched again. "Well, good. Good. I have to go now, Henry. I'm not feeling so grea— *Ah-CHOO!*"

Henry jumped back. "Don't let me keep you!"

Violet slunk back to her apartment. She had never been more embarrassed. *"Ah-CHOO!"* she sneezed. The room seemed to sway and Violet's knees felt weak. She went straight to bed.

That night, she had strange dreams. Waking with a start, she looked out the window. The sky was clear and the moon cast long shadows on the lawn, making the oak tree look twice its size. She closed her eyes and went back to sleep.

"Hel-LO!" Emma shouted as she burst through Violet's front door. "Anybody home?"

Violet blinked. The bright sunbeams coming in her window took her by surprise.

"Good afternoon! How are you feeling?" asked Emma, carrying a tray into the room.

"Is it afternoon?" Violet asked, jumping to her feet. But they were not steady and the room began to spin. She sank back down onto her bed. "Still a little under the weather, I guess," she confessed.

"I brought lunch!" cried Emma, handing her

the tray. It held a bowl of lentil soup, rye toast, and two slices of Swiss cheese. Having skipped dinner the night before, Violet was quite hungry.

"Don't forget dessert," squeaked an unfamiliar voice. Mili popped into the room and put a basket of macaroons on the bedside table.

"Oh, hi, Mili," said Violet, taking a spoonful of her soup.

"I hope you are feeling better," Mili added.

Violet put down her spoon and looked up at Emma. Around her neck was the kerchief Violet had made her for her birthday. Violet straightened up a little. "Thank you for lunch."

"You should get some rest," Emma said firmly, turning to go. Mili followed her out of the room. Violet set the tray aside, then lay back in bed and closed her eyes.

A loud knock at the door woke her. She had just enough time to sit up again before Fernando and Wilbur peered in.

"Violet," said Fernando, "Emma told us you were sick! Here, I brought you something."

He reached into a canvas bag embroidered with his initials. Violet had sewn it for him last year. He pulled out a thermos of hot lemon tea. "To clear your head," he said.

Wilbur was holding something behind his back. When he brought his paws around, a bouquet of marigolds lit up the room. They sat proudly in a vase that Violet had made for him in her pottery class.

"You can borrow it," he said, "until you're feeling better." Wilbur set down the flowers. Then he and Fernando made their way out.

Violet reached for some tea. She looked at the bouquet and remembered how the vase always sat in Wilbur's window, filled with flowers from his garden.

There was another knock. This time, it was Henry.

"Violet! Are you still sick? Oh, you are. I do feel terrible. I wish I hadn't been so gruff yesterday. I am sorry. Here, I brought you something." He reached into his pocket and placed an envelope on Violet's lap. She opened it and pulled out a card with a portrait of Violet on the front. The card said, *Get well soon!*

"I'm not the great artist that you are," he added, "but I wanted to make you something."

"Thank you, Henry. I am already feeling much better," said Violet.

Henry closed the door behind him, and Violet settled in to rest at last. She looked at the things on her bed stand, and a feeling of happiness came over her. She picked up one of Mili's cookies and took a bite. Then she closed her eyes and slept all the way until the next morning.

When she woke up, she hopped out of bed and headed downstairs, straight to Mili's apartment.

"Hello," said Mili.

"Thank you for the cookies," said Violet. "I'm sorry I didn't say that yesterday."

"That's all right," said Mili. "Would you like to come in?"

Violet was surprised at how different Mili's apartment looked. She had unpacked three shelves full of books, two sets of dishes, and several chairs. There were a number of paintings hanging on the wall above the fireplace. And there, next to the window, was Violet's drawing, the one she had made for Mili. The wrinkles had been smoothed out, and it had been placed in a polished silver frame.

Mili saw the look of surprise on Violet's face. "I hope you don't mind! I found it in the hallway yesterday. I thought it looked like a Picasso!"

"Thank you," Violet said, blushing.

Violet and Mili spent the rest of the morning among the boxes, chatting about their favorite places to paint and the best kind of watercolor brushes.

When she got up to go, she looked at Mili. "Welcome to the building," she said. This time, she meant it, inside and out.